Published by Grolier Enterprises Corp.,
Danbury, Connecticut

ISBN: 7172-8192-2

A DISNEY RHYMING READER

GOOFY
THE SPORTSMAN

Fun with Words About Sports

A DISNEY RHYMING READER
GOOFY THE SPORTSMAN

Grolier Enterprises Corp.

"Look!" said Goofy. "A great new store!
It's filled with sporting goods galore.
A baseball bat and soccer ball!
A football, too. I love them all!"

"A bowling ball and bowling pins!
A basketball and swimming fins!
I'll go inside and try each one.
Oh, boy," he said. "Will I have fun!"

Inside he saw a pair of skis.
He slipped them on with graceful ease.
"Ski poles!" he said. "Just what I need
To go downhill with blinding speed."

Goofy said, "I love to ski.
Mountain racing—that's for me.
I'll flash right down this rolling hill
And give myself a giant thrill."

He saw his friends come walking in.
"Good morning, Mickey! Hiya, Min!"
Said Goofy, "Take a look at me!
I'll bet you thought I couldn't ski."

Goofy forgot to concentrate.
He tried to stop. It was too late!
The rolling slope was there no more.
Poor Goofy crashed onto the floor!

Said Goofy, "I have made a mess—
I broke these skis in half, I guess.
I'll have to pay for them, I bet,
And that will put me deep in debt."

Then Minnie said, "That size looks right
For someone who is just my height."
And Mickey said, "They fill the bill.
They'll get you down most any hill."

Then Goofy's friends both waved good-bye
While Goofy found more things to try.
"There's so much stuff," he said with glee.
"This is the perfect place for me."

"A snorkel, goggles, swimming fins.
Here's where my diving life begins.
This wading pool is not too deep.
I'll dive right down and take a peep."

"Through this snorkel I'll get air.
I wonder what I'll find down there.
I hope the water's not too cool."
He ducked his head into the pool.

Donald's nephews came in the store.
They watched him surface with a roar.
"Look!" he said. "This boot's my prize,
And I think it's just my size."

Then Dewey said, "We've seen enough.
We really have to buy this stuff.
We'll dive down to the ocean floor
And bring up treasures by the score."

The boys let out a rousing cheer
And left the store with all their gear.
"Let's go right home and fill the tub,
So we can start our diving club."

Goofy saw a rubber boat,
Filled with air and sure to float.
"I've got a net and fishing pole.
I'm ready for the fishing hole."

Fishing was his favorite sport,
But his cast was slightly short.
"A fish!" he cried and gave a tug.
His hook was in the boat's air plug.

All at once the plug let go,
And the air began to blow.
The boat rose up above the floor.
"Oh, no," he said, "I've lost an oar."

The boat became a rocket ship
That took him on a speedy trip.
"Oh, boy," said Goofy as he flew,
"I'll be in space before I'm through!"

The boat ran out of air at last,
And Goofy said, "That was a blast!"
Donald and Daisy saw him land.
"Goofy," they said, "your flight was grand."

Then Donald said, "This boat's such fun,
We really have to purchase one."
"Right," said Daisy. "It's just the thing
For going camping in the spring."

"Donald," said Daisy, "I can't wait
Until we have our boating date.
We'll paddle down a roaring stream
And make a great exploring team."

Goofy looked around the store
And saw a barbell on the floor.
He bent his knees and grabbed it tight.
"For me," he said, "this weight is light."

"I'll lift it fast! I'll lift it far!"
But Goofy could not budge the bar.
Then Grandma said, "For shame, my boy!
That weight is nothing but a toy!"

She raised the bar and held it high.
"You see," she said. "Easy as pie!"
"Wow!" said Goofy. "You're really great.
How did you learn to lift that weight?"

Grandma said, "From pushing plows,
Baling hay, and milking cows.
But since I've stopped my farming chores,
I'm buying this to use indoors."

"I'll give this baseball glove a try,"
Said Goofy with a happy cry.
The owner said, "I'll pay a fee
If you will come and work for me."

"Sure," said Goofy. "What do I do?"
The owner smiled. "You just be you!
Whoever sees you playing here
Is sure to buy our sporting gear."

Now Goofy's skill is on display,
And people come to watch him play.
That's how our hero came to be
The Salesman of the Century.

How Many of These Words About Sports Do You Know?

Soccer Ball

Football

Fishing Net

Baseball

Fishing Pole

Bat

Glove

Barbell

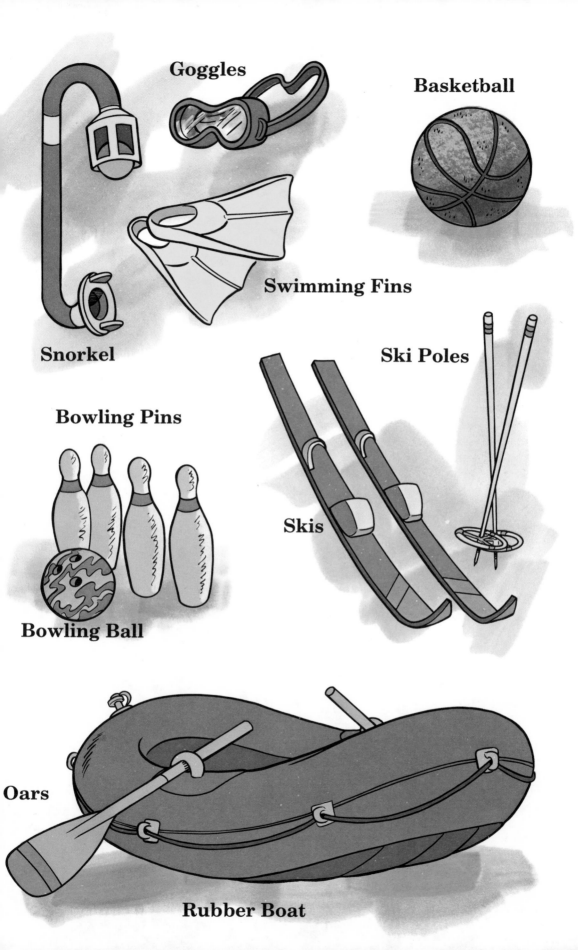

Goggles

Basketball

Snorkel

Swimming Fins

Ski Poles

Bowling Pins

Skis

Bowling Ball

Oars

Rubber Boat